The Three Spires

The Three Spires

Leo Matthews

Pearl Press

First published in Great Britain by Pearl Press

ISBN 978-1-908515-07-0

Printed and bound by Good News Books Ltd, Ongar, Essex, UK

To the people of Coventry and the characters
who inspired this little book.

The Brazen Serpent, to the memory of
Pamela 'Pixie' Coleman-Smith

Foreword

I have been Leo's neighbour for a few years but only recently did I find out I was living next door to a writer! I am delighted to have been asked to write an introduction to his stories.

As an actress I've had to read many scripts and the criteria for the good ones is always the same; interesting characters and a plotline that carries you through to the end. Like good scripts these stories have all the right ingredients.

Basil Sneezby is an unlikely hero but a wonderfully odd and quirky one. He is our link through the adventures, adventures that span time and in the telling touch on many interesting subjects and introduce us to a vivid world of second hand furniture dealers, criminality, church icons and chocolate rolls.

The three stories have an originality and freshness about them which will appeal to a young audience and hopefully we will hear more of Basil and the devious doings of the Hardnuckle family in the future.

Sue Jones-Davies

CONTENTS

The Legacy
Of John Tapley

The minister droned out the last few syllables of the funeral service. Iain Hardnuckle lay dead in the coffin, murdered by person or persons unknown. It was lowered into the grave and the mourners each took a handful of soil and dropped it on top of the coffin; all except for Mandy, his widow. She took a handful of stones that she had previously picked up from the car park and threw them down hard onto the lid. This loud clattering attracted attention to her. People stared with false indignation. Without pausing, she paced off towards the car park, half walking, half running. Without stopping, she ripped off her veil and jammed it into a litter bin and upon reaching her car, she dragged off the long black dress to reveal a colourful summer one underneath. Having removed her mourning clothes, she jumped over the door of her open top Morgan sports car and sped off, showering gravel in all directions.

Iain Hardnuckle was despised by everyone who knew him. No-one was surprised when he was murdered – shot with a flint-lock pistol. Most people, especially Mandy, were glad to see the last of him. The only clue that the police had was the lead pistol ball removed from his body. This ball was fired from a gun with some sort of barrel damage - as the ball passed through it, it had left a distinctive groove in it. Neither the perpetrator nor the gun were found.

Why was he so disliked? He and his brothers owned an antique shop, specialising in old guns - things like shotguns, breach loaders and flint-lock pistols. On top of this, Iain was an underground money lender. That

1

is, he lent money to people at a high rate of interest and never declared the money he made to the Inland Revenue. A good little tax-free earner. His 'customers' were usually desperate people whose businesses were in big trouble and normal loans from banks were not available to them. If they could not keep up the payments, he and his thug brothers would take their possessions instead of cash and sell them in their shop or pass them on 'in the trade'. His poor treatment of Mandy was also legendary. He had never hit her – his cruelty was purely psychological; always wanted to know where she had been, whom she had seen and how much she had spent. If she spent too much he would confiscate the keys to her beloved Morgan sports car. Things were so bad that she went out less and less, even to the point of giving up her job.

Mandy arrived at Basil Sneezby's shop. Basil was a locksmith and he also sold second hand furniture and antiques. She parked on double-yellow lines outside the shop and went in.

'Here are the keys to the house, my dear Mr Sneezby,' she said, handing Basil a key-ring with various keys on it. 'Iain's brothers have cleared out nearly all the stuff but there are some bits left that you can have to sell in your shop. There is bound to be money hidden somewhere. Iain was like that, a miser with squirrel tendencies, so if you find a million quid you can keep it. I don't care, I've got all I want. I'm off to Spain. I've bought a small hotel and I am very well heeled. Here is my phone number, I hope we keep in touch.' Having said that she hugged her 'dear' Mr Sneezby and left.

There was not much time left. Mandy's house had been sold and was to be handed over to the new owners in a day or so. Basil drove to Herbert Goodsur's house in his old van. Herbert was a thirteen year old boy and quite strong, so Basil gave him casual work to help out his 'old bones', as he used to say.

'Come along, Herb! No time to be a slomach!' Basil called through the letterbox. Basil was part Jewish and he would often use expressions that his father used to use. A slomach, I believe, is some kind of slob.

They arrived at the house and as Mandy had said, there was not much left, only some small pieces of furniture. The Hardnuckle brothers dealt

2

mostly with large furniture and what was left was not to their liking. Basil saw that he could get a fair price for it and was quite pleased.

They cleared the house and all that remained was the attic, a job that Basil was dreading. Iain Hardnuckle used to store all sorts of stuff up there and the fact that the Hardnuckle brothers had left it surely meant there was hard work involved. No Hardnuckle in history had liked hard work.

The attic door was locked. It was always locked, even Mandy had never been up there. This was Iain's world, full of his illegal acquisitions. Basil unlocked the door and, to their surprise, there was not much there. There was a writing slope, a tea-chest of ceramics, a small box of coins, another containing small brass things, a beer mat collection, a pile of Sky Blues football programmes, a cigar box full of keys and a roll-top writing bureau. Basil was immediately drawn to the bureau.

'This is a Tapley,' he said in amazement. 'I knew John Tapley, he had a furniture factory here in Coventry. When I was about your age, I used to work for him in much the same way as you do for me. He used to confide in me as if I was an older brother! I was so upset when he died in that awful air raid during the war.' Then Basil looked closer to it and muttered something about recognising this particular bureau.

'See these scratches and dents?' he said, grabbing Herb and indicating to the top of it. 'Let me tell you how they got here,' and went on to tell the story about the bombing of Coventry in World War Two.

The bureau was kept underneath a steel staircase in John Tapley's factory. At the outbreak of war, Tapley's factory was commandeered by the government to make things for the war effort – rifle butts and suchlike. In those days, it was a very young Basil Sneezby who not only did odd jobs for John Tapley, but worked as a messenger boy. He delivered communications to various military headquarters scattered throughout the city.

Basil was out delivering some documents and was nowhere near an air raid shelter when the bombs fell. He took shelter in amongst some rubble; that of the Tapley factory. It was not much protection but he thought it would be good enough to keep the shrapnel away from him while he waited for the all-clear to sound. The bombers had passed over and Basil could see the mayhem in the distance.

3

'Not long now, the all-clear will be sounded soon. How on earth did I survive this?' Basil said out loud, panting in abject terror. The bombs were falling in the distance. Basil peered out from the debris and saw that the storehouse used by Old Mr Hardnuckle, although close to the Tapley factory, was still standing. Then he saw some shadowy figures searching amongst the rubble. It was Old Mr Hardnuckle and his sons (the fathers of the Hardnuckle boys of today), and they were looting! One of the items stolen was the bureau. It suffered minimal damage as it was underneath the very robust steel staircase. Unfortunately, John Tapley was killed in the air raid.

Basil knew that he should inform the police about the looting, but he also knew that there would be reprisals should he be found out. Bearing in mind that the Hardnuckle family had relatives everywhere, including the police force, he decided to tell no-one.

'No time to waste, dear boy!' Basil exclaimed loudly as he shook off this cowl of remembrance. 'We will have to take the top and the back off to get it down the stairs. This is why it has been left here - too much effort to move it!' Basil began to undo the screws on the back of the bureau, hoping the memory of that bombing would go back to where he buried it all those years ago.

The job done, they unloaded back at Basil's shop. The bureau was put in the back of the shop where it would be used for that which it was intended.

'It will remind me of Mr Tapley, the man who taught me everything I know about furniture.' This philosophical statement came as if somehow he needed to justify his intention.

The start of Herb's school holidays saw him at the shop and he and Basil started the job of sorting out all this trash and treasure. Things were priced and put in the shop. All that remained was the writing slope, which was locked and had no key, and that cigar box full of weird and wonderful keys. Like many locksmiths, Basil had a collection of unusual keys, so this box of keys demanded his attention. However, first of all Basil wanted to open the writing slope. It was a simple lock and it only took a few seconds for him to open it. Inside was a ledger listing all the people who owed Iain Hardnuckle money and five thousand pounds in cash. Basil immediately phoned Mandy. In spite of what she had said in the shop, he wanted to do the right thing. Five grand is a lot of money!

'Is that all?' she said calmly. 'I expected more. This is what I want you to do. Burn that ledger and keep the money, it is my gift to you. Don't get all philosophical and call it blood money then give it to the cats' home or something. Put it towards that pleasure boat you've dreamt of,' came Mandy's emphatic reply, so Basil had no choice but to do as she wished.

'At last we can go fishing together, like I always said we would!' came Basil's exuberant shout as he related the gist of the phone call. 'Now, let's tackle that cigar box of keys. Ah, I remember these cigars. They were very expensive. I used to smoke them with John Tapley. I was well under age but in those days nobody took any notice of that. It seemed as though everybody smoked and it was not generally known that it was bad for you. Anyway, the supply dried up and as I didn't like any other brand I decided to stop smoking altogether. How about that – started then stopped smoking before I was old enough to start! Can't get them any more. I think the company went broke or something.'

They stirred through the keys and came across five keys similar to each other. Each had a letter stamped on it and laying them out in alphabetical order they spelled 'Dilly'.

'I think I know what this is all about,' said Basil as he went to put the kettle on. 'This will take a lot of explaining, so I think I need a sugar blast.' He took a chocolate Swiss roll and cut the whole thing up, indicating his intention to eat it all.

'Would you like a trouser piece, Herb?' This was another one of Basil's quaint expressions. It meant the end piece – the one with the most chocolate on it.

'Cor! Yes please!' replied Herb and they sat down while Basil told the story of John Tapley.

John Tapley was an adventurer, he was always working on some exciting project to spice up his life. Perhaps a safari or racing cars and motorcycles. He even had a crack at the land speed record. John Tapley

5

was absolutely stinking rich and he loved to spend! He used to say that if he lived to be one hundred years old, there would not be enough time to spend it all. The Hardnuckles, however, were the total opposite – they were misers.

As Tapley grew older, his body could not keep up with his spirit of adventure. He became too frail for the high jinks of his younger days and had to content himself in other ways. To give you some idea of what made him tick, he once became a local hero when the council tried to close the race track. He told them in a letter that if they closed it, he would set fire to himself on the Town Hall steps. They did not relent and so, come the appointed day and time, Tapley stood on the Town Hall steps and produced a couple of pages of newspaper. By now, quite a crowd had formed. Tapley set fire to these few pieces of paper and walked among the flames. There was not enough flame to hurt anyone or anything and this 'protest' caused a great deal of laughter, not only at this ridiculous stunt but at the council's ridiculous stunt as well. So this was John Tapley: prankster, adventurer, full of the joy of life. It came as no surprise to anyone when he announced in the local paper, The Coventry Evening Standard, his intention to start a treasure hunt – the prize being the Sporian Necklace, a necklace decorated with huge gems.

As with a lot of rich men, there was a facet of avarice to Tapley's character and this idea would not only be fun but would also boost the sales of his furniture. The hunt would work like this. Someone would buy a piece of Tapley furniture and then search all over it for a key. If they found one stuck to it, they then had to track down four more people who had also found one. These five keys fitted five locks on a door at a secret location and the owners of the keys had to solve clues that would lead them to this mysterious door, behind which lay the amazing Sporian Necklace. The first clue was to be printed in the next issue of the paper, just to get the ball rolling. This issue of the paper never went to press because the city was destroyed by the Luftwaffe in that nightmare air raid. This brought an end to the hunt before it had even started and cost Tapley his life. It turns out that the keys were kept in the old bureau, waiting for Tapley to stick them to selected furniture. When the Old Hardnuckles looted the bureau, they found the keys but could do nothing with them; the clues were lost and without these it would be impossible to find the mysterious door. So they were put in the cigar box along with the rest of the keys. Basil knew all about the treasure hunt, he even helped John Tapley to devise some of it, and assumed that the keys were lost in the air raid. He remembered the first clue, 'Go float your boat', but gave no more attention to it. After all, the keys were missing. Over a period of time John Tapley and his treasure hunt were completely forgotten.

They finished their tea and cake. Basil concluded that 'Dilly' had to be a boat.

'What we have to do now is find a boat called Dilly and see where that leads us. Are you up for a treasure hunt, dear boy?' said Basil, knowing that Herb was game for anything, especially if it was an adventure into the unknown.

The first thing they had to do was find out if there is or was a boat called Dilly. Basil knew the Harbour Master at Holyhead, so he phoned him and asked how to find the registered owner, if such a vessel existed. It was not long before Dilly was found. She was 'moored' in a scrap yard, a mile or so from Portsmouth Harbour. Basil phoned the owner, a chap called Bill Burke, telling him he might be interested in buying her. Bill said the last time she was floated was during the Dunkirk evacuation, a trip which caused the engine to malfunction, and was then sold to the scrap yard owner of that time. He and the subsequent owners of the scrap yard all thought that this little boat had a lot of potential and it would be a shame to break her up just for the want of a new engine. Luckily for Basil, nobody had the time or money to fix her up and there she stayed, propped up and neglected, in a scrap yard. The purchase price was very low so Basil said he would drive to Portsmouth and take a look at Dilly.

The duo made ready for a trip to Portsmouth. Neither liked guest houses so it was decided that they would sleep in the van and take camping gear. As it was Herb's school summer holiday and Basil's brother, Firework Fred, would look after the shop, there was no rush to get back. Firework Fred was older than Basil and earned that name by asking for a 'firework' when he wanted a cigar with his pint of bitter. Free

7

of all ties, their adventure began.

Back at the Hardnuckle's shop, the remaining three brothers (Andrew the eldest, then Samuel, and Wally the youngest), were sorting through the last of the items from their late brother's estate. Each of the brothers were collectors. The late Iain and Andrew collected old guns, Samuel was a philatelist and Wally collected posters, kids' comics and newspapers with headlines of historical interest. His prize possession was a newspaper with a headline about the sinking of the Titanic. Among all this stuff was a pile of old newspapers. It was Iain's intention to swap them for a powder horn that Wally had. Obviously, with his murder, this swap never took place. At the end of the day, Wally took this pile of newspapers home and sorted them into title and date order.

It was well known that Wally was the only decent Hardnuckle ever to have lived, and people used to say that the price he paid for being decent was his insomnia. Wally always went to bed very late and always had problems sleeping. His body screamed out for sleep but the kaleidoscope of thoughts would never stop and sleep would elude him. It was no problem for Wally to paw his way through the papers, muttering to himself, 'Alec Douglas-Home, well, well! Gosh, he looks young,' and 'Princess Elizabeth, she's beautiful.'

This muttering and reading went on until 2am. Then, just as he was about to pack up, he saw the article that John Tapley had put in the Coventry Evening Standard. The article proposing his treasure hunt, the hunt that had never started, the hunt that everyone had forgotten.

The following day it was business as usual at the Hardnuckles' shop.

'Bit of activity at the Old Stoat's place,' Andrew said, referring to Basil. 'His brother is running the shop, he tells me he is getting ready to go to Portsmouth and taking the brat with him, wouldn't say any more than that.' Then, in came Wally waving the newspaper with the article on the treasure hunt.

'Look at this! An article on a treasure hunt started by Dad's old enemy, John Tapley. Check out the date, wasn't that just before Coventry was bombed?' said Wally. The brothers were quite intrigued by it. This was all news to them and they wondered if in fact the hunt ever took place.

After some brainstorming, hypothesising and bouncing ideas of varying degrees of stupidity around, they concluded that the Sporian Necklace was still hidden somewhere. So they went to see their father to see if he could shed any light on the matter. Old Mr Hardnuckle was very old, well into his nineties, although his body had yielded to age, his brain was as sharp as it had always been. He read the article and searched his memory.

'Let me tell you what happened. This article explains how the treasure hunt worked. The first clue was to be published in the next issue of the paper but it never went to press – bombed out, you see. Now, I had those keys, they were in that bureau that I 'borrowed' from the remains of the Tapley factory. They were useless without the clues, so I gave them to Iain. The clues died with Tapley, but I wonder if he told Sneezby something while he was devising this thing.'

Still curious, the Hardnuckle boys decided to check out Basil's movements. Maybe all this sudden activity meant something. Perhaps he was on the trail of the Sporian Necklace!

Wally was told to keep watch outside Basil's house and to phone Andrew when they left. Wally was the perfect candidate for this stake-out – no fear of him falling asleep! It was very early the next day when Andrew had the call from Wally. Andrew and Samuel met up and set off for Portsmouth, leaving Wally to look after the business.

It took an hour or so for them to catch up with Basil's old van and they followed at a discreet distance until they reached the scrap yard in Portsmouth. Basil and Herb made contact with Bill, the owner, and he took them to where Dilly was kept. She was propped up in the yard, a sorry sight. She was about thirty feet long, had a small wheel-house and an in-board diesel engine beneath it. Most of the paint had flaked off and the glass in the wheel-house was either cracked, broken or missing altogether. Bill left them to look over her. They went into the wheel-house and almost immediately found some symbols carved into the bulkhead. Could this be one of Tapley's clues? Basil took some paper and placed it against the carved symbols and, pressing hard with his dirty fingers, obtained an accurate copy of the symbols, in much the same way as a brass rubbing would be made. They then left, telling Bill they would

9

return the next day and tell him what they have decided.

They went to a camp-site and after tea they studied the symbols. 'I know these are Hebrew letters but I don't know what this little circle and dashes are,' mumbled Basil, 'and the letters don't form a word. Quite frankly, I'm stumped.' He passed the paper to Herb.

'That little circle looks like the 'degree' thing like in degrees Celsius,' Herb said, wondering if it meant anything. Basil grabbed the paper.

'Yes of course! Look, these letters are OLD Hebrew, they used letters for numbers, same as the Romans did. The letter V was five and X was ten and so on. These letters are numbers, the circle is degrees and these dashes are minutes. This, my dear boy, is a map reference. Tomorrow we'll get a map and see if it leads anywhere.'

Basil was correct, the map reference was for the Isles of Scilly. It was well known at the time when the Tapley family was rich and famous that they had a family crypt on one of the islands. The crypt was emptied after the war as it was considered 'not nice' to have a burial place on such a beauty spot. It seemed logical that this particular island would be a good place to hide the next clue, or maybe this is where the mysterious door with five locks is located. The pair bounced ideas around until late into the night. They decided to buy Dilly and use her to get to the island as there was no ferry service to this tiny fragment of land.

'Kill two birds with one stone, eh, Herb? we get our fishing boat and complete the treasure hunt as well,' concluded Basil, and he put the light out and they went to sleep.

In the morning they bought Dilly. Bill lent them a sanding machine and a few tools and it was not long before the old boat had a coat of paint. With the windows fixed, it was in floating condition. Bill put her onto his trailer and took her to the harbour. There, he reversed down the launching slope. Dilly floated off the trailer and, with the help of a borrowed outboard engine, she putted off to her mooring. By now, Bill was very interested in Dilly and was pleased to let Basil use his workshop. It was only one day's work before he had the engine running like a gold watch. All that remained was the legal side of things, things like insurance and registration and all things boring. Basil and Herb made several trips to Portsmouth and each time the horrible

Hardnuckles plotted their every move.

After some weeks and several fishing trips, the pair became skilful enough to head out to the island where the Tapley crypt was and see what they could find. Arriving at the island they tied up at the mooring and went about looking for the crypt. They found the entrance, which was a steel door locked with a padlock and chain. Basil had brought with him a few tools and some lock oil in a canvas bag. 'I shouldn't be doing this,' said Basil as he took out what he called his 'jiggler' and opened the padlock. They went inside and sunlight streamed in, illuminating cobwebs and dead rats.

'This is minging,' moaned Herb.

'That may be so, but look here! It's a door with five escutcheons in it! This is it, dear boy!' After some fiddling and oiling and a bit more fiddling and oiling the door was opened. It led into a small room not much bigger than a pantry. On the floor was the remains of a pine table with a box on it. Both were eaten away with woodworm and dry rot. Both shaking with excitement, they broke open the rotten box and found the Sporian necklace! Basil took it out into the sunlight to get a better look.

'Hand it over, Sneezby.' Basil looked up and there stood Andrew and Samuel Hardnuckle. Andrew was pointing a flint-lock pistol at them.

'It's loaded and it still works,' added Andrew. Samuel pushed past and grabbed the necklace. Looking at it through a jeweller's loupe he exclaimed,

'It's bling! It's rubbish! Base metal and glass! It's worthless junk!' Andrew gave the gun to Samuel and looked for himself.

'One of Tapley's pranks,' he said in sudden realisation that they had all been HAD! He threw it to the floor and it disintegrated into a million pieces. He grabbed the gun from Samuel, aimed it at the woodworm-ridden lintel above Basil's head and pulled the trigger. With a cloud of blue smoke and a vivid yellow flame, the pistol ball smashed into the lintel, showering Basil and Herb with splinters of rotten wood, dust and dead spiders.

'See you in gaol, Sneezby,' Andrew grunted and the obnoxious pair left.

'Cool,' said Herb, 'I bet no-one at school has ever been shot at.' He extracted the ball from the lintel with the screwdriver and put it in his pocket.

Basil picked up the pieces of the necklace and they both sat on the floor.

'Look at this, Herb.' Basil showed him one of the pieces. 'This piece looks like a key.' He took his wire cutters and snipped around it and yes, it was another key! So they set about looking for another door. It was dark and dusty in there, still smoky from Andrew's gun-shot and it was quite a while before they found the key hole. The door was rendered with plaster, flush with the wall; not at all obvious. The key fitted and with a bit of levering with the trusty screwdriver, the door was opened. Herb picked up the torch and shone it into this room. There was the real treasure, dozens of boxes of cigars: yes, the same ones that Basil and John Tapley used to share before the war. Each cigar was in a wood-lined aluminium tube with a screw top and then put in silver foil-lined wooden boxes. They were as good as the day they were packed!

'I suppose we could start smoking,' grinned Herb.

'No need, ever heard of The Pipe and Cigar Club of Great Britain?' asked Basil.

'Er, no.'

'Well, I can sell these to them for quite a pretty penny. So we haven't done so badly after all.' So they packed up their tool kit and loaded the 'treasure' into Dilly and went home.

Dilly was eventually moored on the Grand Union Canal and the pair made good use of her, becoming a second home to them.

Some months passed and things in Basil's shop were quiet. Herb was there after school, restless and fiddling with that pistol ball, rolling it around on a tin tray.

'Stop that tintinnabulation, boy,' Basil groaned. 'What have you got there?'

'It's that pistol ball from misery Andrew's gun.'

'Let me see,' Basil took the ball and looked at it and then looked again

12

through his jeweller's loupe. 'Look at this: apart from being flat on one side, there is a groove on it. Do you remember what that copper said when he questioned us about Iain Hardnuckle's murder? They were looking for a pistol with some sort of damage to the muzzle. Do you know what I think? I think that his brothers had something to do with his demise; either they provided the weapon or did the deed themselves.' Basil then locked the shop and they made their way to the police station. They both made statements, and the police searched the Hardnuckles' shop where the pistol was found. After some tests were made by the police ballistic experts, it was confirmed that this was the weapon used to murder Iain Hardnuckle. All three Hardnuckles were arrested and charged with the murder of their brother. It turned out that Wally had nothing to do with it and was released. Andrew and Samuel were the guilty parties and went to prison for some horrible length of time. As for the flint-lock pistol – well, the crime was so unusual that it was exhibited in the Black Museum at the Little Park Street Police Station. It can still be seen there today among all the other macabre exhibits.

After the trial, normality returned and Basil and Herb were in the shop. To their surprise, Wally came in.

'Can we talk?' he said nervously.

'Of course,' replied Basil. 'Come into the back of the shop.'

They all sat down and Wally began his speech.

'I have not always agreed with my brothers' approach to business, or indeed the way they led their lives. I have bought out their share of the business and the whole of Hardnuckle Antiques belongs to me. It is my intention to make the name of Hardnuckle respectable. I would like to bury this stupid feud between us forever and I hope we can be allies in the antiques business.'

'Wonderful news!' was Basil's reply. 'Come along, Herb, tea and Swiss roll for Wally and ourselves.' Basil cut up all the Swiss roll, once again indicating his intention to devour it all. 'Wally, would you like a trouser piece?'

'Pardon?' said Wally...

The Icon

Tom Silver, having paid the innkeeper the night before, left early. His breath condensed into billowing white clouds as he walked towards the stables. His mare, Arrow, was well rested and becoming fidgety. The journey from Halstead to Oadby had been tedious due to bad roads and the journey from Oadby to the inn at Barwell was even worse.

Arrow loved to run. She was cross bred to be fast and to possess phenomenal stamina, she stood eighteen hands high and towered over Tom's head. He led her outside and checked her over; hooves, fetlocks, eyes, ears. In fact, every square inch of this huge animal. When he had finished, he tacked her up and set off at a trot. He was travelling light; his only luggage was a leather satchel containing some black bread, beer and a seriously important document. This document was the reason for Tom's journey.

Tom knew these roads well and hoped the road to Meriden would be as good as the last time he travelled it. Time was short and Arrow would have to gallop at least part of the way. They made good progress, the road was smooth with very few pot holes and tree roots to trip the unsuspecting. Tom could feel Arrow's impatience, she wanted to GALLOP, so he kicked her on.

'At last! What kept you, Silver?' she thought.

The sound of her hoof beats changed as she stretched out and began to gallop. Tom leant forward as their speed increased; ducking low branches, holding on as Arrow jumped streams, no view of the road now, only what he could see between her ears!

'Come on Silver, you're not even challenging me!'

Tom released his pull on the reins and the bit fell slack in her mouth.

'That's what I want!' she thought and gave it everything. Her hoof beats changed once more; rhythmic, hypnotic, almost silent as her speed increased even more. All Tom could do was to grip the saddle with his knees and hope to stay on. Mile after mile she kept this up and then their destination was in sight – the monastery at Meriden. Through the wooded part and into the clearing where the monastery stood, fenced off and with a nine bar gate across the drive. Tom pulled on the reins to stop her. His intention was to open the gate but Arrow had other ideas! He let the reins go slack again and hung on; she jumped clean over the gate and refused to stop until they reached the door.

Two of the brothers of the monastery saw this unorthodox approach and assumed there must be a degree of urgency, so they went to their aid. They took Tom to the Father Abbott and led Arrow away to be walked down, fed and watered.

'You must leave here. Soldiers are on their way. Some of your brothers have been imprisoned, others tortured, some even killed.'

Tom handed the document over to the Abbott, it read;

'Dear Father Abbott,

Excuse the lack of formality, there is no time. Soldiers will be upon you very soon. His Royal Highness King Henry VIII has dissolved the monasteries and is taking all land, property and buildings for his own use. You must leave Meriden. Travel light and go to the address shown below, the people there will protect you and look after your needs for as long as you require.

God speed,

Father Duncan.'

Few words were spoken. The monks were assembled in the chapel and given the news. Each went about their assigned tasks, loading just one donkey cart and making ready for their escape. Then one of the monks approached the Abbott.

'What shall we do with the icon?' The icon was in fact a triptych; the main image measured six feet by three, depicting the crucifixion, and on either side were two smaller images measuring about three feet by one and a half. To the right was an image of Mary Magdalene and on the left was the image of Judas Iscariot.

For some strange reason, sometimes the image of Judas would exude tears – it would cry. The brothers felt sure this was a very special icon and did not want it to fall into the wrong hands, or worse, be destroyed. It was too big, too heavy and too time-consuming to take it off the wall and transport it to a place of safety, so it was decided to paint it over with lime-wash (the same lime-wash that was used to paint the walls only a few days before). A thin layer of goose fat was wiped over it first and then the lime-wash was brushed over that. This would make it easier to restore at a later date. It has been said that if you want to hide something you should put it somewhere obvious. Maybe painting over it would be enough to disguise it. Maybe it will be left alone, maybe the brothers could rescue it at a later date. Full of maybe, but this was all they had and having done this, they all left but they never returned.

The soldiers arrived late in the day and they sojourned there to await orders from headquarters. The messenger arrived with their orders. They were to convert the monastery to an army barracks as it 'is of great military and strategic importance'. The monastery was duly converted and became a training camp for recruits. Over the years, the army added extensions and outbuildings. All the time, extra coats of lime-wash were splashed everywhere, including over the icon. The army has a habit of painting things. It was used as a punishment, resulting in everything having a horrible over-painted look.

A century or two passed and it seemed that no one had ever wondered what the three rectangular panels on the old chapel wall were. The barracks outlived its usefulness and was in a poor state of repair, so the soldiers left and the old place became derelict.

✳✳✳

Money was needed to fund some pointless war somewhere and the old barracks was sold to a soldier who had made a lot of money as a mercenary. Matthew Scales wanted to retire from a life of soldiering; it was dangerous and farming seemed a better life for a man of his age. The army had kept the monastery farmlands in full production in order to feed the troops and although now neglected, they lent themselves to being reinstated.

A few years went by and he became a successful farmer, employing scores of local people. He became well respected and even liked by the majority of people.

He married, and when his ninth child was born, thought it was time he built a grand manor house and lived like the gentry. Work began, and when the main part of house was complete, all eleven of them moved in. The old monastery was then taken apart one stone at a time and used to build the stables, laundry and other outhouses of that ilk. Every last piece of stone and wood was used in the building of the new houses – except for our three chunks of lime-wash encrusted timber fastened to the old chapel wall: the icon. The builders thought they were nice pieces of timber and they were stored in one of the outhouses as 'come in handy' wood along with other 'come in handy' bits and pieces. There they stayed for an aeon, or maybe two.

Tempus fugit and the new manor house was passed down through the generations of Scales.

* * *

Lord Scales was the latest occupant of the house. He too had a veritable litter of children and now that photography was fashionable, he thought he should get some photographs taken. Before then, the only way to get images of your family was to pay an artist to paint portraits and with a family of this size, it would have cost a fortune. The new invention of the camera would provide a quick and cheap record of his family. A photographer from London was found and he made the marathon journey from his home in north London to Meriden on his motorcycle and sidecar. He had been a portrait artist and could see that this new technology, called the camera, could cause his main source of income to dry up, which it did. Pre-empting this scenario, he invested his savings in photographic equipment and made a very good living taking photographs, developing, printing and framing. He still painted the odd portrait, as well as landscapes and anything else he felt like, all stored in his shop in various stages of completion – or in his case, incompletion. His shop was a shambles, mainly due to his carrying on two businesses in one small shop, with dozens of canvasses of various sizes as well as old doors and flat pieces of wood on which he could paint something to perhaps sell for a few pounds. His darkroom was also a Heath-Robinson affair, but in spite of all these unfavourable conditions he produced some of the finest work in England.

Meriden was an arduous journey, so he took all the equipment with him so he could finish the job on-site. The negative plates were actually thin sheets of glass, so he packed them in boxes of five with straw in between. With the negative plates as secure as they could be and his tripod roped to the sidecar, he set off.

Having arrived at Scales Hall, as it was now known, he unloaded his equipment into one of the outhouses – the one where our triptych had been stored for centuries, forgotten by all. This was the old, now redundant laundry, so it had a water supply, was reasonably clean and if it were not for the window, would make a good dark room. He looked around for something to cover the window. He saw the centre section of the icon. It fitted a treat and, with a bit of jiggery-pokery, made the place lightproof.

The photography finished, he began to pack up. He looked at the hunk of wood that he had used to cover the window. He wanted to take it back to London and paint a life-size portrait on it. It could be a good earner, but it was too big. However, the other two pieces were manageable and he was allowed to take them back to London. He never had a use for them and they joined all the other mungle in his shop. So there they remained, separated, one piece propped up against the window in Meriden and the other two pieces in the London shop in amongst all the other bits of wood and canvasses.

***

Now that the Second World War had ended, people wanted to get back to normality and Basil Sneezby was no exception. He was discharged early from the RAF after a serious leg injury from a tracer bullet fragment, sustained during an air raid on Manston Aerodrome. He volunteered for military service when he was eighteen and was discharged as medically unfit for duty a year later, just a bit before the war ended. With no prospects of a military career, he decided to follow his other passion – antiques. He mortgaged a shop in Coundon with a flat above it. He stocked the shop with second hand furniture and a few good antiques. He did well. Coventry was being rebuilt and cheap furniture was in demand. As if he did not have enough to do, he worked part time with a locksmith and became well known as a good tradesman.

Everything in his life was rosy, until he caught tuberculosis. His friends and family pulled together and kept his business going until he recovered. He was recovering well and getting bored; he wanted to get back to his business.

'Look at this!' said his mother, waving a newspaper at him. 'Scales Hall is having an antiques auction to fund some roof repairs. You should go, it will test your strength and you might pick up a bargain or two. Kill two birds with one stone.'

'Great idea, Mum. I'm so fed up, I could scream.'

Basil had an old van and he drove to Scales Hall. He bought some small pieces of furniture and some damaged items that he could repair and sell on at a reasonable profit.

At the end of the auction, he carried his prizes to the van. This was his first manual work for weeks and it was very hard going. He sat on the running boards of the van puffing and blowing like an overworked sheepdog.

'Are you alright, sir?' said a refined Yorkshire voice.

Basil looked up and there stood a rotund and very smart figure in a black suit, sporting a wing collar and bow tie. Basil thought he was an undertaker but soon realised he was the butler.

'Yes thanks, I've had TB. I'll be fine.'

'My name is Askham, I'm the butler. I see you've bought the broken furniture that I said would never sell. You restore I assume?'

'Not yet, this'll be my first attempt. I've got few bits and pieces of wood that must be two hundred years old. I can match up and patch up, should make a bob or two.'

'This could be a serendipitous meeting. That outhouse over there is full of rubbish – some of it could be useful to a man like yourself. I need it clearing out. The roofers are coming soon and they want a workshop as well as accommodation. They will use it for both purposes. If you clear it out, you can keep anything you like, you can eat with the staff at the house and there is ten bob in it for your trouble. How's that sound?'

'Deal!' said Basil.

A few days later Basil returned and cleared everything out, stacking the oddments of wood according to size in the van, for ease of unloading. Finding the framing for the poor icon, which was now just twelve pieces of fluted wood with mitres on their ends, he tied them together and put them in the van. By now, he had gained access to the window which was blocked up by the big part of the icon. He carefully removed it and wrestled it to the van.

'What a lovely chunk of oak, very useful – a table top or something,' he mumbled to himself, just like everyone else who had come into contact with it. Just one of those things that has a high 'come in handy' value but somehow never gets used. All this stuff was taken back to the shop and stored in Basil's workshop and like so many times before, the icon was forgotten.

***

Oh, how tempus fugit! Basil wanted to retire. He had done well with the shop and did not owe a penny to anyone. So he decided to make Herb, his employee for many years, the manager of the business. Herb would live in the flat above the shop and have a free hand in the running of the business. Basil would act as a consultant.

So it was. Basil moved out of the flat and into his boat and Herb moved out of his parents' house and into the flat. All was rosy once again!

With Basil away on a fishing trip, Herb decided that a stock take, a tidy up and redecoration was the order of the day. Once that was done, he had a clearance sale. There was so much 'come in handy' (there are those words again) stuff and so many articles stored out in the workshop that the shop was more like The Old Curiosity Shop than Sneezby's Antiques. The damp patch on one of the walls was fixed, and rather than re-plaster he dry-lined the wall with plywood. This became his 'art gallery'. He could knock nails in it and hang pictures – the best way to sell a picture is to hang it. He sold all the pictures in the shop, including the picture of a creepy old clown with a flesh-eating smile, a picture he had hated since he first clapped eyes on it.

When Basil returned, the shop was no longer the cream and green, nineteen-fifties, stuck-in-a-time-warp, scruffy old place, but a bright and attractive shop that was bringing in the customers. Oddly enough, Basil was impressed and felt that his shop was in good hands.

'Look at this Bas,' said Herb, leading him to the new tidy workshop at the back of the shop.

Herb had found the large centre section of the icon and had laid it out on the floor with its frame in position and the two smaller empty frames on either side. The lime-wash had been scratched when Herb was tidying up and he had noticed that there was something painted on it. So he spent a few evenings removing this absolutely gopping (yet another one of Basil's odd expressions) paint. After several cups of sergeant-major's tea and two chocolate Swiss rolls, they decided to finish the restoration and then decide what to do with it.

✳✳✳

Andrew and Samuel Hardnuckle were by now long forgotten along with the brother that they murdered, Iain. Samuel was guilty of being an accessory before, during and after the fact and was jailed for fourteen years. He had served eight of these and was released, and had gone back to the antique shop that was being run by his other brother, Wally. Wally let him live in the flat above the shop and work, as before, in the family business. Samuel was a changed man. Prison can do that, although not always for the better, but in his case he seemed to be more tolerant of people. He visited Basil and Herb frequently when he had something to swap or whatever and he began to actually like them!

Andrew was still in prison. He was the one who had actually pulled the trigger on Iain and was jailed for life. There was not much likelihood of him ever being released but fact is stranger than fiction.

Andrew was summoned to the prison governor's office. He was marched in military fashion by Warden 'Squidger' Lawrence whose face told a story of a thousand street fights.

'Luft, lie, luft, lie, luft, lie!' he bellowed rapidly with a voice like a sixteen-inch battleship gun. One must assume that 'luft, lie' means 'left, right'!

'Hat off! Greet the governor! Speak when you are spoken to! Stand to attention! Don't cross the line on the floor! Give your name and number!'

The governor looked up from a sea of paperwork on his desk.

'Thank you Mr Lawrence. Hardnuckle, there are two things. One, the prison is due to be modernized and the powers-that-be need to release a number of low-risk prisoners to allow the building work to be carried out without the likes of you escaping. Although you are a murderer, they believe you to be low-risk and you will face a parole board soon. If you can convince them that you would be a good citizen, you will be released with conditions.

'Secondly, your wing is the first to be affected so you will move to another wing and share a cell with Derek Croft. He stole and fenced antiques and you sold them, so you have a lot in common. As you have been non-violent, I figure you are less likely to come to blows with him over his personal hygiene. That is all. Dismissed.'

'About face! Quick march! Luft, lie, luft, lie!' Squidger Lawrence once again exercised his sixteen-inch gun of a voice.

Although he was pleased with the chance for release, Andrew was

23

not looking forward to sharing a cell with Dirty Derek. He had breath like a blow lamp and finger nails like a coal miner, his teeth were no more than a row of black stumps, and his body odour was legendary. Pretty grim. Andrew moved into Dirty Derek's cell that day.

The following morning Andrew was wakened by the words:

'Tea, Hardnuckle?'

He looked up and somehow Dirty Derek had produced two cups of tea.

'My sister Mitzi gets it for me, sort of. She lives in France – got her own vineyard. When she visits me she gives me a load of duty free tobacco. I don't smoke so I use it as currency. I can get anything. I've got the makings behind the ventilation grille; tea, sugar, milk powder.'

So, Dirty Derek was a good sort – for a criminal that is! They got on well, except for the pong, the dirty socks in a pile in the corner of the cell and his body odour. Andrew had to do something about it all. But what?

Dirty Derek returned from one of his rare visits to the showers. He had been 'got at' by a group of prisoners. He was given a wash-down with a fire hose and scrubbed with brooms. Back in the cell, he told all to Andrew. Andrew thought that if he could make a gentleman out of him, it would look pretty good at his parole board. It would convince them that this act of altruism meant he would be a good citizen and worthy of release. Dirty Derek was game for it. It was one of those plans where everybody wins. Derek becomes a gent and the abuse stops, Andrew gets his release and both of them get something to do. Prison can be a place of crushing boredom.

Over the weeks, Andrew coached Derek in the ways of the gentleman. How to do a tie up, how to wash and iron clothes, how to eat with his mouth shut, how to eat soup without slurping. The prison dentist fixed his teeth and Derek became Gentleman Derek and Dirty Derek was no more!

Andrew's parole board came and went and he was given his release date. Derek's sentence had almost ended and he had a visit from his sister, Mitzi. She had seen such a change in him that she offered him a job on her vineyard. He was to be released soon after Andrew. Then, after lights out.

'Andy, I have to talk.'

'I'm all ears, Dek.'

'I hate prison, fourteen and a half years in total I've spent in various prisons. I never want to do bird again. But I've got this lock-up in Kenilworth. I own it legit. I have to sell it before I leave here. If I go back to sell it, I will end up in the big house again. As soon as I show up there, my old cronies will come flapping down like vultures. They will offer me easy money fencing some hookey gear, I'm stupid enough to take it and I will get caught and it will be another stretch. Can you sell it for me?'

Andrew thought for a moment.

'Could it be used for a crash-pad? I need somewhere to live. My house was sold when I was banged-up. I've got some money but not enough to buy a house – not at today's prices, anyway.'

'Yes, I used to doss there sometimes. There is a kitchenette and a sofa bed there. I found it ok.'

'Brother Wally is looking for a workshop and storehouse. He deals in big stuff and needs somewhere to store and restore. I'll buy it. After all, it's a roof over me head and it will be better than lodging with a stranger or worse still, lodging with Wally!'

They both laughed and went to sleep. Then, in the morning they agreed on a price and the formalities of the sale were sorted while they were still in prison.

***

Derek and Andrew were playing chess. Derek could not concentrate.

'Counting the days?' Andrew enquired.

'Yeah. AND I've got something on me mind.'

'OK, tell all, Uncle Andrew's listening!'

'When I got nicked, I had a load of hooky stuff in the lockup – the spoils of several burglaries. Among this was a pile of old paintings, unused canvases and lumps of wood. You know the kind of thing, flat stuff that artists like to paint on. They were traced to a photographer's shop in North London. I wanted some well aged oak to disguise a desk I was fencing. I thought that with different drawer fronts nobody would recognize it and I could flog it on. I saw a couple of bits of wood that might do the job, but they were plastered with lime-wash. When I rubbed this horrible crud off, there were pictures painted on 'em. Icons, I think they are called. So I restored them, I figured they were worth a bit, and one of them used to cry. Yeah, a picture of a bloke on it and it used to cry, genuine salty tears! Then the Old Bill came knocking and I got a three year stretch.

'Now, when the Old Bill came to return all this stolen property to their proper owners, they could not account for these icons. They were not on their lists of stolen property, so they reluctantly let me keep them. Truth is, I doubt weather the real owner knew of their existence. They were just planks of wood! Mitzi took them to the lockup and hid them in the loft and I'd forgotten about them. I want you to have them. You gave me a new life – sell 'em for whatever you can.'

After this garrulous discourse, the two friends finished their game of chess in silence.

✳✳✳

Andrew was released from prison and took up residence in the lockup. He found the icons and blanket - wrapped them and put them somewhere safe.

Things went well for the Hardnuckle brothers as well as for Basil and Herb. They did a bit of antique swapping and helped one another on house clearances, and they soon began to trust each other.

Andrew had an old brass lock complete with key, not something he normally dealt with, so he took it to Herb to see if he could swap it for something. He went into the shop and could hear Herb working in the workshop, so he went through.

'So this is the famous workshop that I have never seen!'

'Hi, Andrew,' said Herb, as he wrestled to glue the arm back on a carver chair. That was when he saw the large centre section of our icon and he was gob-smacked. He immediately saw that he had the two missing pieces. The colours, the painting style and the size of the two

26

empty frames were all a perfect match. Andrew fetched the other two pieces and the whole thing was assembled and hung on the wall, hanging for the first time in five hundred years.

It was decided to sell it and share the proceeds and that Andrew was to deal with the sale. He knew someone who was a dealer in such goods – a rather odd and naive but honest character by the name of Czezlaw Horvath, a Hungarian that he had known for some years.

After a few weeks Czezlaw, known as 'Chez' by all and sundry, had found a buyer – an enthusiastic Middle Eastern collector, living in a far-off town with an unpronounceable name. A price was agreed and the icon was taken to Andrew's workshop to be crated, ready for its long journey. The next part of the journey was to take it to a specialist carrier in Birmingham. After all, it was very valuable and needed to be treated with great respect.

It was an early start for Andrew. He was to meet Chez in Birmingham, where the money and goods would change hands. It was cold and foggy at that time of the morning and there was a traffic jam. A copper told Andrew that an artic had jack-knifed and shed its load of scrap metal all over the road. So Andrew took the back road to Four Oaks where he could re-join the main road. As we know, black ice on the road is invisible, Andrew's van skidded on a patch of it and hit a tree. At sixty miles per hour there is no forgiveness from a forty foot oak and that was the end of Andrew.

***

A few days after the funeral, the four boys were back in the old routine, sitting around the table in the workshop drinking tea and scoffing chocolate Swiss roll. The icon had missed the shipping deadline and was back in Herb's shop, and they were wondering what to with it. In came Chez.

'Mornin' all!' he said, looking a bit sheepish.

'Not good news, my friends.' He pulled up a chair and he was poured some tea.

'OK, lets have it,' said Basil with a great deal of finality.

27

'My Middle Eastern customer has jumped ship. He don't want the icon any more, he says there is a curse on it, what with it crying and then Andrew copping it like he did, he got cold feet and pulled the plug. I'm sorry lads but I've got bad vibes with this and I have to say that I can't touch it either. Maybe I am superstitious. Twelve grand is a lot of money, I know, but it ain't worth getting a wooden overcoat for.'

'Twelve grand?' enquired Basil.

'Yes, two cheques for five grand, one to Hardnuckle Antiques and one to Sneezby's Antiques and two grand in cash to help out your cash flow problems.' He paused and looked at four stunned expressions. 'O dear! Andrew's been pulling a fast one hasn't he?'

'He told us he'd got ten thousand pounds,' mumbled Wally. Chez stayed a while and then left. It was clear to all that Andrew intended to keep the cash as well as his share of the five grand. He was still a fiddling reprobate, just like his late brother Iain.

When Wally and Samuel cleared out Andrew's crash-pad, they found a lot more cash, as well as small antiques like jewellery and watches stashed away for subsequent sale without their knowledge. Among all this, they found letters from Derek Croft, it seems Andrew's intention was to rob his brothers blind and then go and live in France with Derek. Who knows what he would have done to Derek and Mitzi?

* * *

The time came for the lads to have their monthly meeting. It was just an informal affair, a time to discuss the antiques business in general – and, of course, to drink tea and eat chocolate Swiss roll. Herb was concerned about the icon, it was still in his workshop and he wanted it out of there.

'This icon has got to go, it has the same effect on me as that picture of a creepy old clown with the flesh-eating smile. I have to admit that I hate it. Any suggestions?' Various ideas of varying stupidity were knocked around and then Basil had one of his eureka moments.

'Have you ever considered who actually owns it? I was given one piece by someone who did not know what it was, and hazard a guess that it was the same for the other two pieces. What was all that lime-wash about? I propose that I research it and find the true owner, and it will probably be Lord Scales.' They all agreed. Herb hated it, Wally and Samuel blamed it for their brother's death and Basil really didn't care what happened to it.

Basil went to see Lord Scales and they managed to unravel some of the mystery. Lord Scales summed up the situation.

'Well, it probably belongs to me as they were given away in error, but I can't prove it. Looking at your photos of it, I think it is a bally awful picture and I would not give it wall space. I'd sell it, but morally it belongs to the Catholic Church and I am not going to jeopardise my reputation. Having said that, it could belong to you because you have it. What a bizarre state of affairs! Over to you, Sneezby – do with it what your conscience permits.'

At that Basil went back to his shop to tell everyone what he thought should happen to it. They gathered around the table and Basil spoke.

'I think we should give it back to the Catholic Church. The monastery at Halstead said they have a space for it in their refectory.'

They all agreed and it was taken to the monastery. They spent some time there just talking to the brothers and the Father Abbot, who suddenly realised that he had some battered old furniture they might like to take away. This was loaded into the van. Then Herb saw the table with no top.

'Hey lads, this only needs a top to be saleable, where can I find a piece wood about six foot by three?'

He was immediately beaten about the head by three men with their caps.

The Brazen Serpent

'Blast this jullahb!'

'Blast these headaches!'

Basil was mumbling under his breath again, as he walked to the chemist shop. The jullahb was yet another one of Basil's quaint old expressions. It is a Punjabi word, meaning diarrhoea. Basil had been unwell for days and it had become so bad that even he had to see the doctor. The doctor had given him some codeine tablets, which would cure things as well as stop the headaches. Basil was in a bad way.

'Blast this jullahb, blast these headaches, blast codeine, makes my head spin, mumble, mumble...'

He did not like his medicine or his illness and he mumbled and whinged his way back to Dilly, his beloved boat, moored somewhere on the Grand Union Canal. He went below deck and prepared to aestivate.

He woke up a few days later feeling much better and, missing his tea and chocolate Swiss roll, thought it was time to pester Herb. Arriving at the shop, he noticed the large wicker hamper that they used to pack the camping gear. It was full and looking ready to go somewhere. Neither of them liked going away on a job, a house clearance or something. Staying in a hotel was a big no-no so they always camped.

Herb explained that the job was in Bude and was taken on by the Hardnuckles but they could not handle the travelling, so they passed the job on to him. A strange job – the house had been derelict since the nineteen-fifties and was being sold by a dying man in a hospice. Very odd state of affairs but the house contained some very interesting furniture, making the trip a worthwhile exercise. Basil thought he could manage to look after the shop, rather than closing it for a day or two, and Herb drove off to Bude.

31

All went well. Herb returned and Basil had coped well with the shop, he was getting better! Herb had divided up the spoils of the deed between the Hardnuckles and himself and the profit was looking good. Basil and Herb unloaded the last of the furniture and all that was left was a couple of doors. They had been replaced by some newer ones that fitted and kept the draught out, and these were put in the shed to be used as firewood. As they were quite old and 'rustic' was the new fashion, Herb thought he could get them caustic dipped to get the fifty coats of paint off and sell them to some trendies.

'Oh no,' said Basil as he looked into the body of the van. 'We seem to have a big lump of wood with a picture on it – AGAIN!'

'Don't worry, Bas. These are being stripped back to bare wood. There is no signature on it and I'm convinced it's valueless. If it was of significance, Hardnuckle would have grabbed it!'

'Oh please, no more adventures.'

After all this heaving, hauling, mauling and mithering of oak sideboards, tables and wardrobes, as well as other 'lightweight' items of that ilk, Basil was feeling decidedly seedy.

After a bit of a break, Basil started to get curious about the painting on the door. It still had it hinges attached so they screwed it to Herb's art gallery wall, the same place where the icon had been hung. With it at head height and with the bright lights on it, they could see that it was really dirty, almost indecipherable, so Herb gave it a quick clean using some Witherden's Patented Picture Restorative.

A very strange picture indeed – it seemed to be a collage of weird symbols, people and animals, strung together on a background of a beautiful garden. In the bottom right hand corner, there was a symbol that neither of them could make sense of. It did not help having a crack in the wood which ran through this symbol.

Herb thought it was a Brazen Serpent.

'You know, that thing from the Bible, the pole with a brass snake wrapped around it. Look, this vertical line is the pole and these bits are the snake weaving around it.'

Basil was not convinced. It did look a bit like a brazen serpent, but why was it there? It was not in the picture and as such was out of place. It seemed very odd.

Basil was still a bit seedy and although it was not cold, he lit the fire in the back of the shop, next to the art gallery. There was a settee there and Basil decided to crash there for the night. Herb went to bed and left Basil to get some rest.

Basil had taken a couple of codeine tablets and although only an hour had passed since taking them, he poured two fingers of his favourite malt whisky and melted into the settee.

'Ah bliss, nothing like a good bagpipe oil.' Bagpipe oil and pills – bad mixture, don't try that at home!

A bit later he woke up to find that the door on the wall had swung to the 'open' position. The room was a bit dark, with only the street lamps and the fire for light, and Basil thought he could see someone in the shadow of the door. The image became brighter and he could now see quite clearly a rather good-looking woman in a long purple dress. The whole image was very much from the early nineteen hundreds. She was sitting sideways on a chair, leaning on the back with arms folded, almost in a slouch. Basil stared in disbelief and then to decided get up and run and not stop until he reached Bedworth. His brain sent messages but nothing happened. I said bagpipe oil and pills were a bad idea. He was not given to panic – he was always calm in a sticky situation, so he did the only thing he could do; he introduced himself.

'Hello,' he said, somewhat slurring. 'I'm Basil Sneezby. Call me Bas.'

She had the kind of beautiful smile that could bring tears to a glass eye. After a bit of hesitation, she spoke.

'Pleased to meet you, I'm Pamela Colman-Smith. Call me Pixie.'

'Are you a ghost, Pixie?'

'No such thing as ghosts, Bas.'

'What are you doing in my wall, then?'

'Buildings have a habit of recording events. They get in the fabric of the building, and when someone has some psychic ability, which you do, and is perfectly relaxed, which you are, they get a fleeting glance of something that happened. People are usually relaxed at night and this is when they see these things, so they think they have seen ghosts. It's nearly always an old building it happens in, so they think it's haunted. I was a spiritual person, I am dead now, and I used this phenomenon to leave you a message. I do have that ability.'

33

'Okay, now I know you're not here to carry me away to Hades, I'll stay and listen.' Not that he could do much else.

'I was an artist and a lot of people made a lot of money out of my work. I, on the other hand, made nothing. I sold some of my best work to pay my rent. I had twelve paintings left. When I got ill, I gave them to my companion, Miss Cork. She hid them in the loft of the house from which this door came. You see, we'd had a break in and some of my paintings were stolen, so she laid them between the rafters in the loft and covered them with some pieces of metal to keep the mice away. Then I died, then she died and I don't know what happened to the paintings. Find them and keep them together as a collection. See that they are exhibited.'

'Okay, I'll do my best. But tell me about the picture on the door.'

'They are the twenty two designs of the Major Arcana that I painted as a collage using a garden as a background. I did it because I was bored, and as I had no canvasses I painted it on the door! I have to go now. Goodbye, Bas.'

'Goodbye, Pixie. So nice to have met you.'

The image faded and Basil was alone again. He thought for a moment and suddenly he realised just what this was all about.

'The tarot cards! Yes, it was her designs! Of course!' Then Basil fell asleep.

✳✳✳

In the morning, Basil had to own up to Herb about having a bagpipe oil so soon after his pills. Then he related the whole story. Herb thought it was a dream, but it did trigger something in his memory. He went to the far-off reaches of his workshop, where he kept a tea chest full of bric-a-brac hidden away as an embarrassment. Stuff that any self respecting antiques dealer would have given to a charity shop, but somehow he never got round to it.

'Found them!' he shouted as he extracted himself from the tea chest.

'Here they are, The Ryder Waite Tarot Cards. Let's have a look...'

They spread them out and as Basil's 'dream' said, the picture on the door was a collage of all twenty two designs of the major arcana. On close examination they discovered that the mysterious Brazen Serpent was on all of the cards as well. It was not a Brazen Serpent, it was Pamela Coleman-

Smith's initials. The elongated vertical stroke was a 'P' and the bits curling around it were the 'C' and 'S'. After a bit more cleaning it was obvious.

'Well, now who's a fool? Brazen Scrpent, my eye. It is a signature!' At those words Basil put the kettle on and cut up another Swiss roll.

***

'Fancy a trip, Bas?'

Herb wanted to buy this old derelict house that he had just cleared out and needed Bas to come with him to help deal with the paperwork and other sundry things that one has to do when buying a house. Herb liked old Victorian buildings and this one had survived untouched from that time. It had no electricity and no hot water supply; its only services were cold water and gas supply. Lighting was provided by gas lamps.

The old man that owned it wanted to sell quickly. His son did not want it because he did not have the time to modernise an old house. Herb on the other hand did not want to modernise it, he wanted to live as a Victorian. This was to be his weekend getaway and retirement castle. Bas was up for a trip and Firework Fred found himself running the shop once more.

They travelled to Bude and met up with the old man's son, a man by the name of Reg Heathfield, who was always in a hurry and always on the boil; hence his nickname, 'Loopy'.

He explained that his father was a criminal and he had bought the house from his partner-in-crime, a much older man by the name of Ian Wainwright. Wainwright had to sell up and go on the run after a bungled break-in.

'That is when Dad got cold feet and bought a new identity and moved to Coventry. He is back down here now in this hospice – got cancer, only weeks left. He's eighty six, not had a bad innings. I know about his wicked past life but he was only eighteen when he met Wainwright. Poor education, no job and ran away from his abusive parents aged fifteen. Not surprising he took to crime, but he is a good man, always looked after me and Mum. As for the house, he abandoned it because if Wainwright got caught, he would have blown the whistle on Dad, no doubt about that! Better to lose a house than your liberty. He bought it in haste and lived to regret it.'

Reg was a solicitor and was dealing with the sale of the house. The four men got on together really well and the paperwork was completed in an atmosphere of relaxed friendship. Only the exchange of contracts was left and that would take a week or so, then the house was Herb's. The old man said it was very strange, signing his actual name of Paul Williams when he had lived as David Heathfield for so long.

$$***$$

Reg contacted Bas and Herb and he told them that the old man needed to see the three of them urgently. So off they went and met at the hospice and, after a brief chat, went to the old man's bedside.

He was hesitant and breathless, then he started to tell the whole, true story of the house and all that went on there.

'I like you pair; that is why I need to tell you about the house. You can back out of the deal after I've told you, if you like. There has been a murder there; that is why I abandoned it. It's true that Wainwright would have blown the whistle on me if he was caught, but the real reason is that there is a body buried under the kitchen floor. If I sold the place, somebody might have found it. I couldn't take that risk, the coppers would have tracked me down. Pierrepoint would have 'anged us BOTH!'

He grabbed Bas' arm with a degree of strength that belied his illness.

'I was only eighteen, it was easy for Wainwright to con me into buying the place and doing a runner. Left me holding the baby, he did.

'Wainwright owned the house and rented it to a couple of old women. One got ill and finished up in one of these places. She was an artist, Wainwright was a thief and I helped him with his break-ins. I could get through small windows, then let him in through a door and we would nick everything in sight. We nicked a load of her paintings and flogged them to a Yank. Made a few quid on that one! We knew she had some more, she told him in idle chit-chat when he went to collect the rent. So when she went in hospital, it just left the other old dear on her own. She told Wainwright she was going away for a day or two, to the coast to take the sea air cure, so we thought it was good opportunity for a break-in. This old dear had no relatives or friends and very rarely went out, she never spoke to anyone. Total recluse!

'We broke in, we hadn't been in there a minute when she came in. Neither of us heard the door, she'd come back unexpectedly! Next thing I know is I'm getting up off the floor. She'd whacked me round the head with her walking stick. I looked round and saw Wainwright standing over her. He'd strangled her, she was dead. We took up the flagstones in the kitchen and dug a hole down until we reached damp soil. Bodies rot very quickly in damp conditions. We back-filled and re-laid the flagstones. The next day we emptied the house of all furniture and personal effects. Nobody asked where she was, nobody asked what we were doing. We emptied the place in broad daylight.

'A day or two passed and Wainwright signed on a merchant ship bound for Australia. He conned me into buying the house. He convinced me that if anything came to light I'd be in the clear. So I bought the place and he had money for a fresh start in Australia. It cost me every penny I had.

'I found out many years later that he had fallen in with a really bad crowd and was involved in an armed robbery. There was a shoot out and people got killed. They hanged the lot of them. Wainwright got what he deserved, he was despicable.

'Meanwhile, I moved into the house and I got a job as a butcher's boy. Could not pay the bills, so I had to start working evenings in the pub. I was exhausted, then the nightmares started. Kept dreaming about the old lady that Wainwright killed. So I was working from eight in the morning for the butcher, then going to the pub for early doors, then going back again in the evening and what with the disturbed sleep, it was all too much. It was killing me. I decided to do a runner. I wrote to Cyril Hardnuckle – I'm sure you know the Hardnuckles. During the war, he and Iain had pinched some documents from a bombed-out house during an air raid. There was a birth certificate belonging to a bloke about my age. He was dead, so I became Dave Heathfield. They rented a room out to me and they wanted a lot of money for this false identity, so I worked for old Hardnuckle until I had paid off this debt.

'Then the Alvis factory started to take on more workers and I landed a job there and worked my way up to charge hand. Earned good money, got married, bought a house and the rest you know. I told my wife about my past, the change of identity, everything, but never told her or anyone about the house.' He grabbed his oxygen mask and had a few lungs full and lay back on his bed. Nobody said anything.

Herb decided to go ahead with buying the house but first he needed to sort out the police and suchlike. The police were informed and they exhumed the body from the kitchen. The old man made his peace with the law; made his peace with his family and then made his peace with his maker.

***

Normality returned, which is always a bad sign, and Basil was looking after the shop. Herb had taken ownership of the old house and had spent a few days there, giving it a really deep clean. It was late in the afternoon when he arrived back at the shop.

With all the goings on they had completely forgotten about Basil's 'dream', and Herb had not been able to get into the loft. He needed their three-extension ladder to get up there. The hatch was over the stair well, a daft place to put it, and Herb was gagging to get up there.

After a lot of talking, several inches of Swiss roll and several pints of tea, Basil's curiosity had been stimulated and he was keen to see the old place again and see if there really were twelve paintings hidden in the loft. A few days later, Firework Fred was duly bribed with cigars and beer and once again found himself in the shop and Basil and Herb set off to Bude once again!

The ladder was wrestled into position and Herb scampered up, taking with him their extra-bright inspection lamp. To his surprise, there was nothing up there. The pair went into the loft and made their way to the other end where they saw some bits of metal, enamel adverts and the like laid neatly across the rafters. Feverishly, they moved them out of the way and found twelve oil on canvas pictures, neatly wrapped in calico. After a while, the shock of finding them wore off and they duly took them back to the shop to decide what to do with them.

The duo had a reputation for doing the right thing, usually resulting in them not making any money, but for once they came out on top. Herb, being a smart cookie, decided to lend them to an art gallery and they in turn would lend them to another art gallery and so on. The pictures were on the road! All this lending would attract one thing for Herb – royalties! A nice little earner for him, but more to the point, Pixie's art work was kept together and being shown to art lovers who knew that Pixie's signature was not a Brazen Serpent.